KINDERKITTENS

Show-and-Tell

by Stephanie Calmenson
Illustrated by Diane de Groat

Scholastic Inc.
New York   Toronto   London   Auckland   Sydney

To Anna Smeragliuolo
—S. C.

To Pepper
—D. G.

ISBN 0-590-46349-7

Text copyright © 1994 by Stephanie Calmenson.
Illustrations copyright © 1994 by Diane de Groat.
All rights reserved. Published by Scholastic Inc.
CARTWHEEL BOOKS is a registered trademark of Scholastic Inc.

12 11 10 9 8 7 6 5 4 3 2 1   4 5 6 7 8 9/9
Printed in the U.S.A.   24
First Scholastic printing, August 1994

THE
KINDERKITTENS

TEACHER:
MS. CALICO

"Who would like to sing 'Three Little Rabbits'?"
Ms. Calico asked her kindergarten class.
"Me! Me! Me!" answered the Kinderkittens.

Sophie jumped up and started hopping like a bunny.
Nikki started hopping, too.
Then Stanley joined in.
Suddenly the whole class was hop-hop-hopping.
"As soon as everyone sits down, we can start to sing,"
said Ms. Calico.

It took a little time, but finally the Kinderkittens were ready.

Three little rabbits hop, hop, hop
Up a hill to the top, top, top.

A *fox pops up on the other side.*
Three little rabbits hide, hide, hide!

Ding, ding! The school bell rang. It
was time to go home.

"Remember, we have Show-and-Tell tomorrow," said Ms. Calico. "If you have something to share, please bring it to school."

"Wait till you see my dinosaur!" said Nikki. "It glows in the dark!"

"I'm bringing my talking Moon Man," said Stanley. "I got him for my birthday. What are you bringing, Sophie?"

"I don't know yet," Sophie said.

Everyone had something exciting for Show-and-Tell. Sophie wanted to bring something exciting, too. But what?

Sophie's mommy came to the door. "Hi, Sophie," she said. "How was school today?"

"It was fun," said Sophie. "Do you want to see me hop like a bunny?"

"Sure," said Sophie's mommy.

Sophie hop-hop-hopped right out the door.

Mommy smiled. Then she asked, "Do you have any homework?"

"I want to bring something for Show-and-Tell tomorrow — something exciting!" said Sophie.

"Maybe you'll find something at the park," said Mommy. "Would you like to go there for some ice cream?"

"Oh, yes!" said Sophie. She wanted to get to the park fast. She stopped hopping and started skipping.

"Hello, Sophie," called Bessie from the ice-cream truck. "What flavor would you like today?"

"Strawberry, please," Sophie said.

"Coming right up," said Bessie.

Sophie sat down to eat her ice cream. The sun was hot. The ice cream was melting fast. Sophie tried to lick it quickly. But she wasn't quick enough. Ice cream dripped everywhere.

"Mmm. That was good!" said Sophie when she finished.

"I'm glad you liked it," said Mommy. "Now I think you could use one of these."

Sophie's mommy held out a napkin. But the breeze blew it away. Sophie chased the runaway napkin.

"Got you!" she cried when she caught it. She waved it in the air.

On the ground in front of her, something else waved, too. It was something big and dark. Sophie knew just what it was.

"Look, Mommy!" cried Sophie. "I found my shadow."

Suddenly Sophie had an idea. It was a Show-and-Tell idea. And it was exciting!

"Shadow, would you like to come to Show-and-Tell with me? It will be fun!" said Sophie.

She took a step closer to her shadow. Her shadow took a step back. Sophie took another step. Her shadow did, too.

Sophie ran after her shadow. But her shadow was as fast as she was.

"Wait for me!" called Sophie. She ran and ran, but could not catch her shadow. When she turned the corner, her shadow disappeared.

At home, Sophie tried to find something else for Show-and-Tell.

"I could bring my pet goldfish," said Sophie as she watched him swim back and forth in his bowl. "He's nice. But he's not very exciting," she decided.

"I could bring Mommy's new pot holder," she said. She held it up and made believe she was talking to the class. But there wasn't much to say about a pot holder — even one shaped like bananas.

Sophie was disappointed. She could not find anything as exciting as her shadow. And her shadow was nowhere to be seen.

The next morning at school, Ms. Calico asked, "Who has something for Show-and-Tell?"

"Me! Me! Me!" cried many of the Kinderkittens.

Ms. Calico called Stanley up first.

"This is Moon Man. He can talk!" said Stanley. When Stanley pulled a string, Moon Man said, "Greetings, Moonbeams."

Everyone clapped for Stanley.

Sophie sat quietly and watched the other Kinderkittens take their turns.

Nikki was the last to be called. She held her dinosaur up in front of the class.

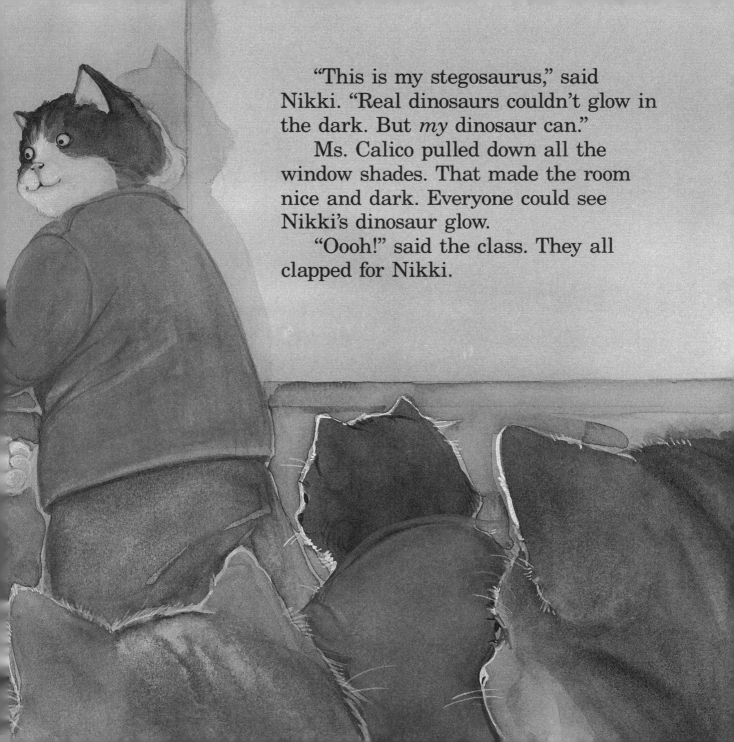

"This is my stegosaurus," said Nikki. "Real dinosaurs couldn't glow in the dark. But *my* dinosaur can."

Ms. Calico pulled down all the window shades. That made the room nice and dark. Everyone could see Nikki's dinosaur glow.

"Oooh!" said the class. They all clapped for Nikki.

"That was a very good Show-and-Tell," said Ms. Calico. "Nikki, would you please pull up the window shades near you?"

Ms. Calico went to pull up the shades at the back of the room. *Boom!* Something fell. The Kinderkittens turned around to see what it was.

"I didn't see that can of paintbrushes in the dark," said Ms. Calico.

Just then the sun came shining into the room through the other window. That's when Sophie saw it. On the floor. Right behind her.

"Ms. Calico! Ms. Calico!" cried Sophie. "I have something for Show-and-Tell!"

Sophie stood up, but she did not walk to the front of the class. She did not want to lose her shadow again.

"This is my shadow," said Sophie.

Sophie pointed to her shadow. Her shadow pointed, too. Sophie danced. Her shadow danced. She twirled. Her shadow twirled.

"Where's *my* shadow?" asked Nikki.

"I want one!" said Stanley.

"I want one! I want one!" said the other Kinderkittens.

"Sophie has a shadow now because the sun is shining right on her, and she is blocking its light," said Ms. Calico. "When something blocks light, a shadow is made. I will show you how it works. We will have a shadow parade."

"Hurray!" cried the Kinderkittens.

Ms. Calico got out a flashlight and set up a big screen. Then she pulled down the shades again.

"Sophie, you may be the leader," said Ms. Calico.

Sophie held her arms out like an elephant's trunk. The rest of the Kinderkittens followed.

Then it was Nikki's turn. She started hopping like a bunny.

That gave Ms. Calico an idea. "Who would like to put on a shadow play?" she asked.

"Me! Me! Me!" answered the Kinderkittens.

The class picked a play and practiced hard. Soon they were ready.

"The Kinderkittens proudly present *Three Little Rabbits, A Shadow Play*," announced Sophie.

When the room was dark, they began.

Three little rabbits hop, hop, hop
Up a hill to the top, top, top.
A fox pops up on the other side.
Three little rabbits hide, hide, hide!
  Ms. Calico clapped and clapped. The
Kinderkittens were very proud.

Sophie was the proudest Kinderkitten
of all. She took a bow. Right behind her,
Sophie's shadow bowed, too.

THREE LITTLE RABBITS
A Fingerplay Song
by Stephanie Calmenson

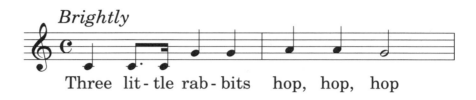

Brightly

Three lit-tle rab-bits hop, hop, hop

Up a hill to the top, top, top.

A fox pops up on the oth-er side.

Three lit-tle rab-bits hide, hide, hide.

HAND SHADOWS

You can make these hand shadows of a rabbit and a fox. In a darkened room, shine a light on a white wall or screen. Hold your hand in front of the light, as shown.

SHADOW PUPPETS

To make these shadow puppets, trace the shapes onto a dark piece of heavy paper. Glue the puppets onto flat sticks.

SHADOW FRIENDS

Hang a piece of paper on a wall. Have a friend stand in front of the paper. Ask someone to shine a light on your friend. Then trace your friend's shadow. It's your turn next. Color in your shadow pictures.

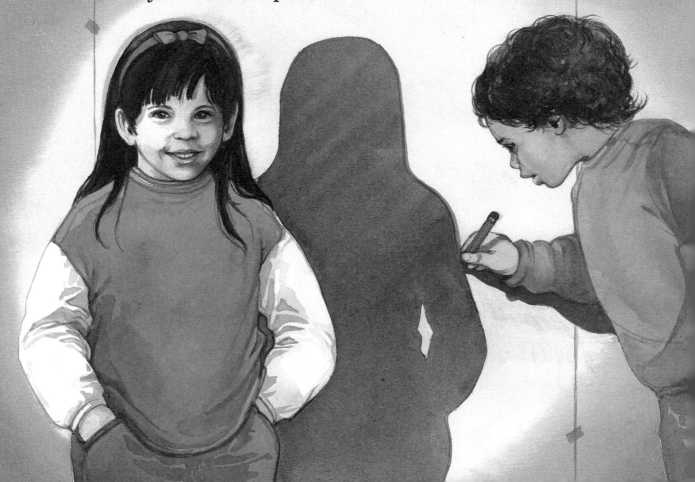